The Prank

Nate's Journal

The Prank

by K.E. Calder

Vanwell Publishing Limited

St. Catharines, Ontario

Vanwell Publishing acknowledges the financial support of the
Government of Canada through the Book Publishing Industry
Development Program for our publishing activities.

Vanwell Publishing acknowledges the Government of Ontario through
the Ontario Media Development Corporation's Book Initiative.

Vanwell Publishing Limited
P.O. Box 2131
1 Northrup Crescent
St. Catharines, ON
Canada L2R 7S2
sales@vanwell.com
1-800-661-6136

Produced and designed by Tea Leaf Press Inc.
www.tealeafpress.com

Printed in Canada

National Library of Canada Cataloguing in Publication

Calder, Kate, 1974–
    The prank / K.E. Calder.

(Nate's journal)
ISBN 1-55068-115-X

    I. Title. II. Series: Nate's journal (St. Catharines, Ont.)

PS8555.A46515P73 2003   C813'.6   C2003-905467-5

For Jaimie Nathan
a true friend

Journal of Nate Brown

DO NOT READ

—

THIS MEANS YOU!

September 2 ◉

My life sucks.

Today was the first day of grade eight.
Good stuff that happened: none.
Bad stuff that happened: too much to write down.

My mom gave me and my sister a bag of school supplies. What does she think we need with crayons? My sister, Tammy, is in grade six and I'm in grade eight. Not grade two. Grade eight. I could see giving us markers. Or even colored pencils. Maybe a highlighter. But crayons?

She also gave me new pens, a ruler, and this notebook. I'm going to use it as a journal. Just for the record, this isn't a diary. There is no lock or little golden key. It is not pink. It's just a plain notebook.

Anyway, back to today. I have to share a locker. Kids in every grade eight class before this year got their own lockers. I get to grade eight and what happens? We have to share. We have the biggest grade eight class Emery Public School has ever had. Just my luck.

I share a locker with Frankie Caricci. He stuck a mirror to the inside of the door. He uses it to fix his hair. First, he pushes all his hair forward with his hands. Then he messes it all up again. Then he makes it stick up along the middle of his head.

Our skateboards take up a lot of room in the locker. I hope Frankie doesn't plan on keeping a lot of stuff in there.

Suki and Ashley share the locker right beside ours. I've known them since grade two. They do everything together. This summer they went to camp. They were counselors in training. Big deal. They can't stop talking about it. Ashley gave me one of her rope bracelets. She made them at camp. She tied it on my wrist. I wonder how long I have to wear it.

There's a new girl this year. Her name is Miranda de Silva. She's the best-looking girl this

9

school has ever seen. She has long, dark, curly hair and brown eyes. Today she was wearing a cool skater T-shirt. Her locker is down the hall by Trevor and Jason's. I was standing at their locker talking to Jason. Miranda was putting books in her locker. She looked over at us, so I said hi. She said hi back.

Then Trevor ran up behind me and pantsed me. He ripped my jeans down to my knees. I was standing there in my underwear! I swung at Trevor, but he stepped out of my reach. I couldn't exactly chase after him with my pants down. I bent down and pulled them up as quickly as I could.

Trevor and Jason bent over laughing. A couple of kids shouted as they walked by. Miranda smiled and then covered her mouth with her hand. Trevor is so dead.

It's a good thing I wasn't wearing my white underwear. The ones with all the holes. I had on the black ones that go down my legs a bit. I should throw those holey underwear out, though. You never know when you're going to get pantsed.

September 3 ☼

After school

It's only the second day of school. Things have gone from bad to worse. I got called down to the principal's office. I was on my way to third period. Mrs. Berger was waiting for me in her office. Frankie and Ramesh were there, too. Ramesh was sitting on the shiny green sofa by the wall. Frankie was in the big brown chair in front of the desk. I looked at them. They just looked back. I sat down beside Ramesh on the shiny green sofa.

Mrs. Berger was behind her desk. She took off her glasses. She wears her hair in a big ball on top of her head. It makes her look like she has a freaky tall head.

"Boys," she said. "The janitor saw you skateboarding in the hall yesterday." I wanted to roll my eyes, but I couldn't. She was looking right at me. It was skateboarding as usual.

Mrs. Berger gave us the same old speech. On school property we have to carry our boards. Blah,

blah, blah. We've heard it all before. Why do adults hate skateboards so much?

She said, "Stay off your skateboards on school property. Next time I'll take them away." She said some more, but I wasn't really listening. When she was finished, we went out in the hall. Frankie put his pencil case on top of his head. He said in a high voice, "Stay off your skateboards on school property. Next time I'll make you eat them!"

Frankie and I aren't worried. We still have a place to skateboard. We've been hanging out at Ramesh's place a lot. He lives in a huge house. His father built him this cool skateboard ramp. It's the biggest ramp around. It takes a few of us to drag it out onto the street. Tons of kids always show up with their boards. I wiped out about a week ago trying to do a 360. I cut my elbow. It was all bloody. It was pretty gross. I ruined my new sweatshirt. I didn't tell Mom about that. I hid it under my bed.

ramp

Third period was music class. This year we get to play instruments. Everyone picks an instrument on the first day of school. I really wanted to play the trumpet. But I was in the office, so I missed the beginning of music class.

By the time I made it to class, I was out of luck. The class had picked their instruments. They were all sitting in rows. Frankie took the last cool instrument. It was a saxophone. Trevor and Jason were sitting in the middle row with their trumpets. There were no more trumpets left.

The only instrument left was a flute. I asked Jason if he wanted to trade. Of course he didn't. I had to take the flute. Then I had to sit in the front row with all the girls. No guy would choose the flute. I am the only loser guy in the front row. I'll be playing the geeky flute for the rest of the year. The girls all whispered when I sat down. It totally sucked. I noticed I was sitting beside Miranda. Today she was wearing another skater T-shirt. She looked great. Hi, I'm Nate, the loser flute guy.

The music teacher is Miss Mirel. She said we have to play solos for the final test. I'm going to have to play my flute in front of the class. I turned around and looked at Trevor and Jason. They both pointed at me. They looked like they were going to explode with laughter. I'll never live it down.

September 4 ☿

5:00 p.m. — The gym

I'm trying out for basketball. Well, I was. Now I'm sitting on a bench. Trevor will make the team for sure. He's the best player in grade eight. I thought it would be cool if Trevor and I were both on the team. I didn't make it past the first cut. I hardly got a chance to dribble. I can't blame the coach for cutting me. I'm not the greatest ball player. And that's putting it mildly. But most of the guys here went to basketball camp all summer. How can I compete with that?

I'm just waiting around for Trevor now. We're going over to Jason's house after tryouts.

September 5 ᴧᴧ

5:30 p.m. — My bedroom

I'm grounded. I can't leave my room until I have
put away all my stuff. I am only allowed to come
out to go to the bathroom. I've gone to the
bathroom five times since I got home from school.

My mom is so picky. Why does she care if there
is stuff on my floor? It's MY room. Why does
everything have to be so neat? Who cares? She gets
so worked up about it.

When I got home from school today, she came
in my room. She bent forward and told me to look
at her head. So I did.

She said, "What do you see?"

So I said, "The top of your head."

She said, "What's on it?"

I said, "Hair."

"What color is it?" she said.

"Brown," I said.

"And what else?" she said.

I didn't know.

"GRAY!" she shouted. "Gray! You're giving me gray hair!" She was really starting to lose it.

So I just stood there and didn't say anything.

Then she yelled some more. "Pick up your clothes! Put your books away! Put your games away! Do it! Now! Don't leave this room until it's done." Then she slammed my door, and I heard her stomp down the stairs.

That was an hour and a half ago. I put some stuff away. But I'm going to need that stuff again tomorrow. That's my point. Why put things away? I'm just going to bring them out and use them again! It's a waste of time.

I told Trevor I would meet him at the basketball court. I'm supposed to be there at six o'clock. I can't put all this stuff away in less than half an hour. There's too much. I can't even see the floor. It's just one big sea of pants, socks, T-shirts, and comic books.

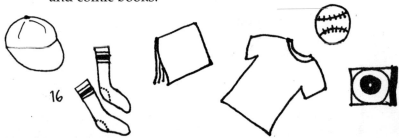

Doh! I just picked up a pair of pants. A piece of cold pizza fell on the floor. I think that's from three nights ago.

Mold

Gross. I just had a bite. I'll probably die from food poisoning now. It'll be my mom's fault. It'll be on the six o'clock news. Boy, twelve, was trapped in his room and had no choice but to eat three-day-old pizza.

None of this stuff will fit in my drawers. There are already lots of things piled behind my door. My closet is too full. It's jam-packed with stuff. There's a solid wall of junk inside. When I open the door, it stays there. I can't even take anything out. The whole load of stuff will fall into a messy pile. I know this for a fact. I tried to pull out a badminton racket last week. It wasn't pretty. It took me an hour to get everything packed in again.

There simply is no place to put this stuff. At this rate, I'll just have to sit in this mess until I get old and move out.

5:59 p.m.

I'm at the basketball court. Clothes and comics are under my bed. Rest of pizza is in my belly. Feeling kind of sick. There's Trevor. Time for some hoops.

September 6

1:30 p.m. — The backyard

Today I went to this cool skateboard park. I went with Jason and Ramesh. It's at a school yard downtown. Jason's mom drove us there.

The whole yard is a bunch of paved hills. I wish our school had paved hills! There were all sorts of other skaters there. They were all doing these wicked hard tricks. This one kid was really good. Jason told me that he goes in competitions.

We skated for about three hours. I want to go back there every weekend.

September 8 ☺

9:49 p.m. — My bedroom

Frankie and I waited around after school for Ramesh. We wanted to go back to his house and use his ramp. Mrs. Berger saw us sitting by the sidewalk. We were holding our boards. We weren't doing anything wrong, so she just looked at us. We just sat there and looked back. She couldn't say anything about our boards. Ha.

Then she got in her tiny green car. It's the same type of car Mr. Bean drives. The ball of hair on the top of her head was smushed against the roof. She honked at us on her way out of the parking lot. It sounded like a squeaky toy. She waved as she left the parking lot. We waited until she was around the corner. Then we started laughing.

We waited for a while, but we didn't see Ramesh. He must have left the school through the back doors. I told Frankie about the

skateboarding park. He wants to go and check it out. Maybe we can go next week. Nothing beats the school yard. Maybe that good skater guy will be there again. I want to ask him how he gets into competitions.

Ashley and Suki came out the front doors. They asked us where we were going. We said nowhere. They said they were going to the mall. They asked us if we wanted to go, too. I didn't want to. But Frankie decided to go with them. He said he needed to buy new warm-up pants because he lost his. The girls laughed when he said that.

Suki said, "Reeeeeally?"

Frankie said, "What?"

And they both said, "Nothing."

They are so weird sometimes.

The three of them went to the mall. There was no way I was going with them. I just skated home. Well, I stopped at the park on the way back to my house. I did a perfect 360 off one of the steps. Of course no one was around to see it.

If a train is traveling from point A to point B at a speed of x...

WHO CARES?!?!

September 9

Math class

I am supposed to be working on a word problem. I hate word problems. So I'm doodling in my journal. No one can tell what I'm doing anyway. My journal is inside my workbook. I can't believe I have never thought of doing this before. I can read another book or write in my journal. The whole time my teacher thinks that I'm doing math. I can't believe other kids don't do this.

Mr. Sweet asked Miranda to do a problem on the board. She's up at the front writing it now. Her hair is in two curly balls on the sides of her head. None of the other girls do that with their hair. She is so cool.

Trevor just threw an eraser at me. It hit me right on my cheek.

I said, "Hey!"

He said, "Sorry."

This is the longest math class in history. Why do we even have to know this stuff anyway?

21

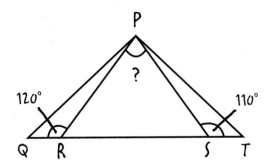

180 − 120 = 60

180 − 110 = 70

60 + 70 = 130

180 − 130 = 50

Still in math class

That was close. Mr. Sweet just walked by. He was walking around behind me. I had to switch to math stuff on the spot. Good thing he didn't look too closely. I was just copying the question that Miranda was doing. As I was saying, not doing math during math class is great. It has saved me from death by boredom.

Ugh. Mr. Sweet just yelled at Trevor and me for talking. It wasn't even my fault. Trevor leaned across his desk. He asked me about the prank. He wanted to know if I had any ideas.

Every year the grade eight guys at Emery Public School pull a giant prank. It has to be better than the year before. Last year the grade eights put a tire around the flagpole. No one knows how they put the tire around the top of the flagpole. Maybe someone climbed to the top. That would have been hard carrying a tire. Jason says they probably had a crane, but I don't think so. The janitors couldn't figure out how to get it off. Finally they just had to cut the tire.

A few years ago some guys put plastic wrap on the toilets. Even the ones in the girls' bathrooms. Once, someone let a pig loose at the Halloween dance. None of us were there. But we heard that all the girls were screaming. The teachers couldn't catch it for about half an hour. No one knows who did those pranks either.

I have no idea what we can do for a prank this year. I just know that it has to be good. Those pranks are hard acts to follow. I mean, where the heck do you get a pig?

We have to decide soon. We have to do it by Halloween. They always pull the prank on Halloween. It's a guys-only thing.

Coming up with a great prank is the easy part. The hard part is doing it without the teachers finding out. They know that something always happens on Halloween. They'll be on the lookout.

Uh oh. I think Mr. Sweet can tell that I'm not doing math. He's coming this way.

If a train is traveling from point A to point B...

September 12 ☺

8 p.m. — My bedroom

I'm grounded again. Everyone is over at Ramesh's house. Not me. I have to stay at home for the whole night. Mom looked under my bed and in my closet. She found the mess. I was supposed to clean it up, like, a week ago. She freaked out. I can't leave the house until I put my stuff away. Properly.

So far tonight, I've played some games on the Internet. I played checkers with some kid in England. I'm probably not supposed to be on the Internet. I think Mom thinks I'm actually cleaning my room. I would clean it, but there isn't anywhere to put all my stuff. Well, except for under the bed and in the closet. Maybe I'll try tomorrow. I don't feel like cleaning up tonight.

Tammy just came into my room. Without knocking, I might add. She wanted to borrow my skateboard. Ha! Yeah, right. I told her she doesn't even know how to skateboard. She says she's going to start. I told her to forget about it.

September 15

4 p.m. — Detention

I got a detention today. It was totally worth it. It happened in music class. We were all playing our instruments. Trevor and Jason were laughing at me. I can't blame them. I look like a fool sitting there with all the girls. There I am, playing the dumb flute! I was trying not to pay attention to those jerks. I wish I played drums instead.

As I said, I sit beside Miranda. She's already really good at the flute. So I try to pretend that I like playing it, too. That's not easy. It's really hard to play. Also, it makes me look even more like a loser. When Miranda is not looking, I pretend to break my flute on my knee. You know, just so the guys know that I hate it.

They were really bugging me today. Jason and Trevor kept playing air flute. They were also making loud kissing sounds. They started saying that I'm going to play flute at band camp. I wanted to knock them upside the head with my flute.

 26

There's something really gross about the flute. You play for a while, and then you tip it sideways. All this spit comes out the end. It's really gross.

Miss Mirel turned around to write some notes on the board. It was the moment I'd been waiting for. I turned sideways and leaned back. Then I emptied out the flute spit onto Jason. He was the closest. He freaked out and jumped out of his chair. He had goober all over the front of his jeans. Everyone in the class started laughing.

I turned back around. I almost jumped out of my chair. Miss Mirel was standing right in front of me. She scared the you-know-what out of me. She looked really mad. I stopped laughing.

All she said was, "Nate, detention."

The rest of the class stopped laughing, too. The girls in the front row flipped through their flute books. I looked at Miranda. She was looking at her book and trying not to smile.

So I got a detention. I don't care. I made Miranda smile. She thinks I'm cool now. I guess I got those guys pretty good.

7 p.m. — My room

My mom has totally lost her mind. When I got home from school she was waiting for me in the hall. I could tell she was mad about something. She asked why I didn't come straight home from school. I told her it was because I had a detention. That made her even more mad. She told me to go up to my room. So I did.

There was nothing in it.

Well, there was my bed and my dresser. But that was it. The bed was bare. There were no sheets on it. The dresser was completely empty. There was nothing on top of it. The drawers were open, but there was nothing in them. My desk was completely bare. Even my computer was gone.

My closet doors were open. But the closet was totally empty. There was nothing under my bed. Nothing in my dirty clothes basket. Nothing behind the door.

Nothing.

I started to panic. Everything was gone. I ran downstairs. "Mom! I've been robbed!" I yelled.

"No, you haven't. You've been cleaned out," she said calmly.

My EMPTY room

"What?" I said. I didn't understand. What was she was talking about? I thought Trevor and Jason were playing a joke on me. Paying me back for the flute spit. Maybe they had hidden all my stuff.

"Come with me," my mom said.

So I followed her. We went outside and she opened the garage door. There, against the back wall, was my room. Everything. It was all in boxes. Clothes, books, and video games. Comics, medals, and stuffed animals. Baseball bat, roller blades, and skateboard. Everything. I just stood there.

"I thought I'd get you started," she said. "There are some empty boxes in the corner. Any stuff you don't want you can put in the empty boxes. The rest you can carry up to your room. Then you can put it away properly."

"But—" I started to say.

"No buts." She always says that. No buts. We walked back inside.

My dad was in the living room watching the news. He turned around in his chair. "You'd better get to it, Nate," he said. He turned back around.

I've brought six boxes of clothes up to my room so far. It's taking forever. I have to put all my clothes in the drawers and on hangers. I can't believe this. Whose mother does this? No one's.

September 16

9 p.m. — The garage

Where are my gym shoes?!?! I've looked through about fifteen boxes and three bags of stuff. I can't find them anywhere. (But I did find my Tamaguchi. I lost that years ago. It's dead now.)

Today I had gym class, and I couldn't find my shoes. I felt like a nerd. I tried to look for them this morning. But I was going to be late for school. I didn't really want another detention. Not for something boring, like being late.

When I got to school, I looked in my locker. It's packed with stuff already. My stuff. Frankie doesn't keep anything in it besides his mirror. It's completely packed with my books and clothes and old lunches. Oh, and our skateboards. It's stuffed right up to the top. I searched through everything. My shoes weren't in there. Then my locker door wouldn't shut. That almost made me late for gym class. By the time I got there, class had started. Everyone was playing basketball.

So I had to play basketball in just my socks. I kept sliding all over the place. Ashley and Suki asked me what happened to my shoes. Suki tried to help me think of places where they could be. Then Ashley hit her and gave her a dirty look. What was that all about?

Ashley said I could borrow her extra shoes. As if. I wouldn't be caught dead wearing a girl's shoes. She must have huge feet.

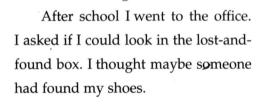

After school I went to the office. I asked if I could look in the lost-and-found box. I thought maybe someone had found my shoes.

My shoes weren't in there. Of course. But I did find my winter mitts. The ones with the half fingers and tops that fold back. I thought those were gone.

As I was leaving, I peered in Mrs. Berger's office. There was Miranda. She was with her parents. They were sitting on the green couch. She was sitting on the chair. Mrs. Berger was sitting behind her big desk.

Miranda looked up and saw me looking in. What was *she* doing in the office?

September 17 ≋

After school I waited outside for Ramesh. I sat down on the little hill by the sidewalk. I was sitting on my board because the grass was still wet. It rained earlier today.

I saw Ramesh coming out of the school. I stood up and picked up my board. As I was running down the grassy little hill, I dropped my board. It rolled all the way down the hill. Then it rolled into the giant puddle at the bottom. The board went right under water.

Ramesh laughed. I tried to reach it, but I couldn't. There was nothing I could do. I had to walk into the puddle to get it. My shoes got completely wet. I ran out of the puddle. Water came out of my shoes.

Great. I have no gym shoes, and now my regular shoes are wrecked, too.

"I have to go home. I can't skate with puddles in my shoes," I said. Ramesh left and I started to walk to the sidewalk. I couldn't stand the soggy feeling, so I took off my shoes.

Just then Mrs. Berger drove out of the school parking lot. She pulled up beside me in her tiny little car. She rolled down the window. "What happened to your shoes?" she asked.

"They're wet," I said. I held them up for her to see. They dripped water.

She sighed really loudly. "Well, you can't walk all the way home in your socks. Get in. I will drive you," she said.

She was right. I couldn't walk all the way home in socks. It was a good twenty-minute walk to my house. So I went to the other side of the car to get in. My socks were soaked. They started to drop off my feet. If they weren't dirty before, they were now. Little rocks on the ground dug into my feet. I let out a little "ouch" with every step I took.

I stood beside her car. I had shoes in one hand and my board in the other. She rolled her eyes and popped the trunk. I put my skateboard inside it. Then I flopped over to the car door and got in. I put the wet shoes on the floor in front of me. She looked down at them. I guess I should have put those in the trunk, too.

It felt funny to be in such a tiny car. It felt even funnier to be in Mrs. Berger's tiny little car. I told Mrs. Berger where I lived. We started driving to my house. I looked quickly at the ball of hair on top of her head. It was touching the roof of the car. Then I looked out the window. I didn't want her to see me staring at her weird hair.

I didn't say much. I just answered her questions. She asked me how I like grade eight so far. I said fine. She asked me if I like my teachers and classes. I said yes.

As we were turning onto my street, she had a sneezing fit. She couldn't stop. She sneezed about twenty times. Her eyes were closed tightly. She had to pull the car over to the side of the road.

Then she said, "I hab a coad." She asked me if I would open the glove box. There were tissues in there and she needed one. I opened the glove box. A bunch of stuff popped out onto my lap. A map, sunglasses, some mail, and an extra set of car keys.

"Oh goodness. Sorry about that. That glove box is far too small," she said.

I gave her a tissue. Then I put all the stuff back into the glove box. She blew her nose. It made a loud honking noise. I almost laughed out loud.

I told her which house was mine and she pulled up in front. Tammy was in the driveway on her roller blades. She waved at Mrs. Berger. Mrs. Berger waved back. I thanked her for the ride home. She said I was welcome. I picked up my wet shoes from the floor of her car. They had made a little puddle. I got my board out of her tiny trunk. Then I waved good-bye and went in the house.

Tammy followed me in, of course. Seeing me in Mrs. Berger's car freaked her out. She wanted to know what happened. Ha, too bad. I hope wondering about it drives her nuts.

I walked up the stairs to my room.

My mom yelled, "Nate, work on your room!"

Yeah, like I could forget.

September 18

11:45 p.m.

The plan just hit me! I can't believe I didn't think of it before. It's still a month before Halloween. We'll have time to plan everything out perfectly. I just called Trevor. His mom answered. Her voice was quiet, like she had been sleeping. She asked me if I knew what time it was. She sounded mad.

She said, "It's almost mid—"

Then Trevor picked up another phone and said, "Mom, I've got it." She just huffed and hung up her phone with a beep.

I told Trevor my idea. He thought it was cool. We'll need Ramesh, Jason, and Frankie to be a part of it. We talked about the plan for about half an hour. Then my dad came into my room. He told me to get off the phone and go to sleep.

I can't sleep. I keep thinking about the prank. I run it over and over again in my mind. There's a lot to do. We need some help, though. This is going to be the best prank ever.

September 19 ☼

Today, Frankie, Trevor, and I went to Hilldale High. It's two blocks from Emery Public. It's where we'll be going when we get out of this joke of a school. We had to go and talk to Frankie's older brother, Monty. I've never talked to him before. But I've seen him. He has his own truck. He always has a new girlfriend. Anyway, we had to ask him to help us with the prank. We need someone who can drive. Someone with a truck.

We walked up Cherry Street and across Birch Avenue to the high school. A bunch of high school kids were on the sidewalk. They all looked at us as we walked toward them.

"Come on," said Frankie. "We've got to go around back to the auto shop." We walked past the kids. I tried not to look any of them in the eye.

I heard one of them say, "What are they doing here?"

We looked like little kids, and they looked so much older than us. I hope it's not like that next year. I hope we're all bigger by then.

We walked around to the back of the school. A bunch of girls were practicing field hockey. We stopped and watched them for a minute. We'll have to do some major growing if we want to get with high school girls.

We kept walking to the far side. There was a metal fence around a small parking lot. Cars were parked all over it. Some were missing all the wheels. Some had no doors. Some had no windows. A lot of them were rusty. Frankie walked up to the gate. It had a chain through it and a padlock. He shook the gate, and the chain rattled loudly. Frankie yelled, "Hey! Monty!"

Trevor and I looked around. No one came. Frankie yelled again even louder. "MONTY!" A guy in blue coveralls poked his head out of the door. He had a white bandanna on his head.

"What do you want?" he called over to us.

"Get Monty," Frankie said loudly. I thought the guy would come over and pound us. He just went back inside. Monty stepped outside. He was wearing jeans and a black T-shirt. His black hair was long and tied back in a ponytail.

39

"Frankie! What are you doing here?" he yelled.

"C'mere!" Frankie yelled back.

Monty came over to the fence. He unlocked the padlock. Then he let us into the parking lot. Frankie told him our idea for the prank.

He thought about it for a minute. Then he said, "Yeah, that's cool. I never got to pull a prank in grade eight. Mrs. Berger found out about it before we could go through with it."

I said, "What were you going to do?"

He said, "We put the emergency sprinkler system on a timer. You know, so everyone would get soaked when the lights went on. But Mrs. B. caught us in the act."

I said, "Too bad, that would have been classic."

Monty said he'll help us. But he says we have to get everything ready. We have to make sure the coast is clear. We have to get the ramp. He says we can't screw up. He says if he gets caught, we're in big trouble.

"We can do it," said Frankie. "Right guys?" He looked at me and Trevor.

"Yeah, right," we said. At least I hope we can.

September 22

I came right home from school today. I found a note taped to my bedroom door.

ANYTHING LEFT IN THE GARAGE WILL BE PUT IN THE TRASH. YOU HAVE TWO WEEKS.

Great. I have to put away the rest of my stuff.

September 23

6:45 p.m. — The garage.

There is still a lot of stuff in here. I don't even know where to start. When I got home from school today, Mom was in the kitchen. I didn't even put down my bag. I just came straight out to the garage. I'm getting used to spending time in here. Maybe I could start a garage band. But the only instrument I play is flute. Forget that.

I've been reading a book for French class for an hour. At least I'm getting my homework done.

41

September 24 ☺

5:15 p.m. — The garage. Again.

Today was a P.D. Day! I love P.D. Days. They are almost as good as snow days. Snow days are better because of the surprise factor.

Tammy went to a friend's house. My mom wanted me to stay and clean the garage. Then she decided that I couldn't be home alone all day. I don't know why. I've been staying home alone for over two years. Doesn't she trust me? She said that she called Jason's mom. She said I was to go over there for the day. I wasn't about to complain. She dropped me off before work.

When I got to Jason's house, things got even better. Jason's mom said she had some shopping to do downtown. So, she dropped us off at that great skatepark. The one in the school yard downtown! We skated for hours!

That kid who is really good was there. He told us about a competition. It's called Skate Max. It's going to be at another skatepark across town. He said there will be an eleven-foot ramp. There are also mini ramps and a street course. It sounds really cool.

September 25 ⅔

12:30 p.m. — The lunch room.

I told Trevor, Frankie, and Ramesh about Skate Max. They are down with it. I can't wait. We're all going to practice as much as we can. Going in a competition is one thing. But if one of us won, that would be totally cool.

Suki and Ashley asked if they could sit with us to eat lunch. That was weird. They never want to sit with us. Ashley just asked what I'm writing. I told her, "None of your business."

September 29 🌀

One week left to get my stuff out of the garage. I guess I should start working on that. Maybe I'll do it tomorrow.

October 6 ☺

One week later

I finally got the rest of my stuff back into my room. It took all day yesterday. Mom said I should have thrown out a lot more stuff. How could I? None of it is junk.

I still can't find my gym shoes. Now my favorite gym T-shirt has gone missing, too. I thought maybe it was lost in the garage. But I didn't find it in all that stuff. Maybe it's buried at the bottom of my locker. I'll check tomorrow.

I couldn't go anywhere until Mom looked at my room. She looked under the bed, in the closet, and behind the door. She even looked behind my dresser. Everything is in its place. She called Dad up to see. Neither of them could believe it. Tammy even poked her head in my room. She couldn't believe it, either. Mom gave me a big hug and said I did a good job. Dad slapped me on the back and said, "Looks good." Then he said that we were all going out for ice cream.

That was my prize for cleaning up my room. Eating ice cream with my dad, my mom, and my little sister. IN PUBLIC.

We went to the Dairy Bar beside the mall. Mom and Dad wanted to sit at one of the tables outside. Dad ordered a jumbo banana sundae. It took him forever to eat. About ten kids from my school walked by us. Some of them were with their parents, too, so they could hardly laugh.

And then who walks by? Monty Caricci and his girlfriend. He saw me and said, "Yo! Frankie's friend. How's it goin'?"

So I said, "Cool."

Then he held his girlfriend's hand, and they went inside.

My mom said, "Who was that older boy, Nate?" She said it really loudly.

"He's just a friend," I said.

"How are you friends with him?" she said.

"He's Frankie's older brother," I said. I was done my ice cream cone. The rest of them were taking forever to eat theirs.

"Frankie Caricci?" said Tammy.

Like it's any of her business.

"Yes. Can we go? Are you guys almost done?" But they weren't done. It took an hour (or five minutes) for them to finish.

9:30 p.m. — My room

I just looked up Skate Max on the Internet. It says, "Skateboarders of all ages are welcome. Put your skills to the test. All pros and amateurs are invited. Sign up now."

There will be judges and everything! They watch you while you skate the ramps. They look for skill and original moves. There is also a prize for best trick of the day. There is a raffle, too. They give away skateboards, T-shirts, and skate shoes. (I could use some new shoes!) AND there will be a punk band, rappers, and DJs.

I wish I had heard of this competition before. I can't wait.

October 7 ☀

I totally emptied out my locker. Again. My T-shirt was not in there. I even went to the lost and found at the office again. Nothing. I looked for my shoes while I was there, too. They weren't there either.

But I did find my headphones at the bottom of my locker. I've been looking for those.

In music class, Ashley and Suki were whispering. They kept looking at me. I couldn't take it anymore. I asked them what they were talking about.

Suki said, "We heard you guys have a plan for a prank."

Who told her that? That stuff is top secret. I can't even write the details in my journal.

I asked her who told her. She said, "Frankie."

Frankie? I'm going to talk to that guy later on. Who does he think he is?

"What are you going to do?" asked Ashley.

I said, "I'm not telling you two anything. Forget about it!" They begged me to tell them. Finally, Miss Mirel told them to be quiet.

Then Miranda leaned over. She whispered in my ear, "What's the Halloween prank?" It's the first time she has really talked to me. I could feel her breath on my ear. It was warm. I turned my head to whisper back to her and we bumped heads.

She said, "Ow!" really loudly and put her hand on her head.

Miss Mirel turned around. She looked at me and Miranda and then turned back to the board. Jason and Trevor were laughing quietly behind me.

I leaned over slowly. "It's a joke. The grade eight guys do it every year. It's always on Halloween. It's always something different. You have to come up with something cool. Cooler than the grade eights the year before."

She said, "Oh. So what are you guys doing?"

I wanted to tell her. I really wanted to tell her. She would have thought it was so cool. She would probably brag to the other girls that I had let her know and no one else. And that the plan was all my idea. We would probably become boyfriend and girlfriend. And it would be cool for Miranda to be my girlfriend.

But I can't tell her the plan. If she told the other girls, then the whole school would find out. Besides, the guys would kill me.

THE PLAN: TOP SECRET

So I just said, "Sorry, I can't tell you. It's just that it's top secret."

"Oh." And that was all she said to me. She didn't seem too upset that I wouldn't tell her. I was thinking of maybe giving her a little hint.

I wanted to ask her what she was doing in the office that time. But I guess I'll have to wait.

Miss Mirel told us to pick up our instruments. We all played the notes that she had written on the board. It turned out to be "Baa Baa Black Sheep." We sounded like a bunch of dying animals.

October 8

1:30 p.m. — Math class

I asked Frankie why he told the girls about the prank. He said he likes Suki, and he wanted to talk to her. He thought that the prank would be something to talk about.

"Yeah, that's something to talk about all right!" I said. "Something to talk about to the whole school! Do you know what will happen if the teachers find out it's us?"

Frankie just stood there. He hadn't thought of that. "I can ask them to keep quiet about it," he said.

I said that it was probably too late. Something like that is just too juicy. Suki and Ashley are friends with all the girls. And girls have big mouths. Sooner or later, the whole school would find out. It wouldn't be long before the teachers found out. If the teachers found out, they'd be on us like glue. We wouldn't be able to pull off the prank. Or worse, they would catch us in the act. That's the last thing you want. To be caught pulling the prank.

And we could sure get in a lot of trouble. Not that this prank would hurt anything. Or break the law. Or even break any property. I just think we'd be in a lot of trouble.

4:15 p.m. — The kitchen

Frankie went and talked to Suki and Ashley. He said they promised to keep quiet about the plan. He seemed pretty sure about it. I have no idea how he's making them not tell anyone. He said he made a deal with them. Well, whatever deal he made, I'm just glad it worked.

All the kids are talking about the prank now. They know that someone is planning something. They just don't know it's us.

51

October 9 ~~~

8:15 a.m.

I had the best dream last night. I was at Skate Max. I was in the competition. It was just me and that really good skater guy. The one I met at the school yard downtown. The ramps were greased with oil. It made me go really fast. At first I was scared. But I got used to it. I started pulling off all these wicked tricks. I was getting tons of air.

Then my alarm went off.

6 p.m. — My bedroom

My room is too neat. I can't find anything anymore. All my comics are put away. I can't find the one I wanted to read. I needed my allen key to fix a wheel on my roller blades. It's put away. Everything is put away. When I want something, I have to go looking for it. I like my things out in the open. That way I can see them. I hate opening drawers and closet doors.

October 10 ✓✓✓

This morning at school I found a note. It was lying right in the middle of the front hall. I picked it up and looked around. There was no one else in the hall. It was a copy of a list. It was a list of five boys' names. My name was on it. It was fourth from the top. Frankie's name was first, then Ramesh, then Trevor. Jason's name was last. Some of our names had checkmarks beside them. What is up with that? It was a girl's handwriting, too. It was all round and bubbly. There were little pictures of balloons and hearts.

Later, I asked Trevor if he knew whose handwriting it was. He didn't know.

I tried to look at Suki's handwriting during French class. She thought I was copying her, so she hid her notebook. Ashley leaned over and whispered that I could look at her paper. So I did, but it wasn't the same writing as the list.

I wonder if fourth from the top is good or bad. Is it boys they like, or boys they don't like? What else could it possibly mean? What about the other boys in class? Why are our names the only ones on the list? It's driving me crazy.

I asked Frankie what he thought about the list of boys' names. He said girls are always making lists like that. He didn't know if the list was good or bad. He said it must be a list of the coolest guys in school. Yeah, right. He just thinks that because his name is first.

After school we went to Ramesh's place to do tricks on his ramp. He was wearing his older brother's shoes. He can't find his. Jason's zip-up sweatshirt has also gone missing.

I think someone is stealing our stuff. First my shoes and then my T-shirt. Then Ramesh's shoes and Jason's sweatshirt. I have no idea who it could be. Who wants our stinking gym clothes?

October 11

Hi Nate,

Your journal was really fun to read. I liked the part about the list of boys' names. By the way, I know what the list was about. It's boys who are nerds. Ha ha. I have a good idea for the Halloween prank. You should all come to school in your underwear. That would be really funny.

TTFN,
Tammy.

October 12

10 p.m.

 Tammy is so dead. I can't believe she read my journal!!!! Who does she think she is?!?!

I don't know what I'm going to do, but I'll get her back. She's always doing things like that. Last year she had a sleepover party. She let her friends in my room. They hung out on my bed and looked at all my stuff. I told Mom and Dad. Tammy got in trouble with Mom for that. There is no point in ratting her out about this. Mom will just say that we're too old to be tattling.

Besides, I'd rather get her back in my own way. Mom would be way too easy on her. I guess I'll also have to be careful about the plan.

Tammy, if you're reading this you can stop now. I'm not going to say what the plan is. And you'd better watch your back. I'm planning something for you, too. Ha ha to that! Just go back to whatever it is you do for fun. Go play with your Barbie dolls or something.

HA HA ha ha ha ha ha

October 14 ★

I have to think of a costume for the Halloween dance. I don't even want to wear a costume. But you have to dress up. The teachers won't let you into the dance if you aren't. The last time I went trick-or-treating was three years ago. I can't believe we have to dress up.

Jason thinks it would be funny if we all came as big chickens. I think it's a dumb idea. Where are we supposed to get big chicken costumes? Trevor said we can wear each other's clothes and come as each other. That's a dumb idea, too. All our clothes look the same. The teachers won't believe that we're dressed up.

I thought we could all be vampires. Jason says that's so overdone. Who cares? It's easy and cool looking.

I talked to Miranda in music class today. It was the end of class. We were cleaning the spit out of our flutes. I asked her what she thought she would be for Halloween. She said she hasn't thought about it yet. I guess it is still kind of early. But it was the only thing I could think of to say. Then I remembered that time in the office. So I asked her why she had been there.

She said that Mrs. Berger thought she should go to another school. I couldn't believe it! I asked what she had done to get kicked out of school. She said that she wasn't being kicked out. Mrs. Berger told her about another school. A school for gifted students. She's gifted! You must have to be pretty smart to go to one of those schools. I didn't even know there were schools like that.

She told her parents that she doesn't want to go. She said she's just starting to make friends at Emery. And she really likes it here. That blew me away. I didn't think anyone really liked this school.

I'm really glad she's going to stay. But I didn't tell her that.

October 16

I was walking down the hall on the way to music class. I could hear Jason and Trevor laughing. I thought that the whole flute thing wasn't funny anymore. So I asked them, "What's so funny?"

"Do you and your sister share clothes?" said Trevor. They both laughed even harder.

I turned around. There was Tammy talking to a bunch of her little grade six friends. She was wearing my good soccer pullover. The one I got for Christmas. The arms were too long for her. She had them rolled up. I walked right up to her.

"I want my shirt back," I said. Her little friends all looked scared.

"It's not your shirt. I found it," she said.

"What? It is too my shirt, Tammy. You know it is," I said.

"Nuh-uh. I found it in the garage a couple of weeks ago. You didn't want it anymore," she said. I wanted to scream.

"Tammy! You know all the stuff that was in the garage is mine."

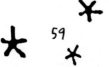

"Mom says you don't care about your stuff. Or you would take better care of it," she said.

"Well, Mom is a nut!" I yelled. "That pullover is mine, and I want it back! Or else I'll tell you-know-who that you like him."

"You don't know who I like," she said.

"Oh yes I do," I said.

"How?" she said.

Without missing a beat I said, "I read it in your diary."

Her face went completely white. Her friends looked at her, then at me, and then back at her. I had her. She couldn't say anything. She couldn't even freak out that I read her diary. After all, she knew that I knew she read my journal.

"You'd better not say anything," she said in a quiet, shaky voice.

"As long as that shirt is back in my room after school," I said. I gave her a big smile.

"Fine," she said.

I walked away. It's a good thing she didn't ask me where I found her diary. I had no idea where it was. I didn't even know that she had one.

October 17

I still can't find my gym shoes. I had to play badminton in just my socks again. Trevor and I got paired up with Suki and Ashley. They kept laughing and making faces at each other the whole time. It was really bugging me.

After classes, Suki was waiting for me at my locker. When I got there, I started opening the lock. She just stood there, leaning against the locker. Staring at me.

"What?" I finally said.

"Did you have fun in gym today?" she asked. She had a goofy look on her face.

I said, "Not really." I took some books out of my locker. I started putting them into my bag.

She was still standing there. She was just staring at me. Then she said, "Did you like playing badminton with me and Ashley?"

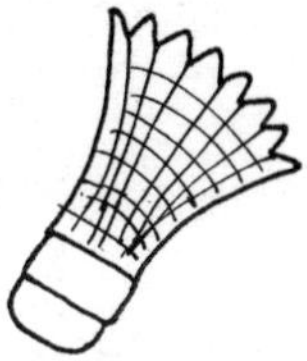

"Uh, yeah, I guess so," I said.

"Ashley always hit the birdie to you instead of Trevor." she said. "Did you notice that?"

"No she didn't. She mostly hit them into the net or out of bounds," I said. I wondered what she was talking about.

"Yeah, but she was aiming for you," said Suki.

"Oh," I said. I closed my bag and tossed it over my shoulder. "Okay, well, see ya," I said. I pulled my skateboard out of my locker. I shut the lock and turned to go home.

"Nate, I know someone who likes you," Suki said quickly.

I turned around. "What? Who?"

I wondered if this had anything to do with the list. I pictured Miranda in music class. I thought of her laughing after I poured flute spit all over Jason. Maybe Miranda had written the list. Maybe it was a list of guys she was in love with. Maybe now my name had been moved to the top.

"Guess," said Suki.

"Miranda?" I blabbed out. Then I wished I hadn't said it.

"Miranda?" She laughed a little and shook her head. "No. Guess again," she said.

"I don't know," I said. I didn't really want to play this guessing game with her. "I give up. I don't care." I started to walk away.

"Ashley," she said.

"What about her?" I said.

"She likes you, dope," said Suki.

"What? Does this have anything to do with the list of guys' names?" I said.

"What list?" she said. She clearly had no idea what I was talking about.

"Never mind," I said. "I'll see you later." I turned and started to walk away.

"Nate?" Suki called out after me.

"What?" I said.

"But Ashley likes you. What should I tell her?" she said.

Why was she asking me? I didn't like Ashley. "I don't know," I said.

Suki and Ashley kept looking at me in music class.
They wouldn't stop whispering. I knew they were
talking about me. I couldn't stand it anymore.

I said, "What are you guys talking about?"

Suki said, "What's the prank, Nate?"

I said, "I'm not telling."

"Then we're not telling you either," said Suki.
She whispered in Ashley's ear. They both laughed.

Miranda and I had to share our music book.
She didn't say much to me. I wonder if Suki told her
that I thought maybe she liked me. I wonder what
Suki told Ashley. I wonder what that list is about.
One of them must have written it. They must have
changed their handwriting. I wish my name wasn't
on that list. I can't stop thinking about it.

Not that I care, but I think I'm getting better at
the flute. I have to try when I'm sitting beside
Miranda. I don't want her to know that I think the
flute sucks. She really likes the flute.

October 30 @

10 p.m. — Bedroom

The Prank — Operation: Keys.

The first part of our plan has been completed.

Today Trevor had basketball practice after school. He waited until the coach was getting in his car. Then he ran up and asked for the keys to the supply closet. He said that he forgot to put his basketball away. The coach was in a hurry, just as Trevor was hoping. He gave the keys to Trevor. He said that Trevor could give them back to him in the morning. Score!

Trevor went into the supply closet. He put his basketball away. Then he got on his bike and went to the hardware store. Jason and I were there waiting for him.

There were five keys on the key ring. Trevor knew which one was for the supply closet. We didn't know which key unlocked the doors beneath the stage. That figured. We should have got the keys cut weeks ago. We could have tried them out to make sure they worked.

We really needed the key for the stage. We weren't sure which key was which. So, we got all five keys cut. It cost $6.75 between the three of us.

The guy at the hardware store looked at us kind of funny. He was older than us, in high school.

He said, "What are these for?"

I said, "Locks."

He said, "What locks?"

I said, "Why do you want to know?"

He said, "Because they look like school keys."

Busted. The three of us just stood there. He could tell we were up to something.

I tried to act like it was no big deal. "Yeah, so?" I said.

"What school do you guys go to?" he said.

"Bishop Street Public," I lied.

"Cool," he said. He went to work and made the keys for us.

I'm the official key holder. I will be the one meeting Frankie at the back doors. So it makes sense for me to have the keys.

October 31 ☺

4:35 p.m. — Back doors of the gym

Operation: Ramp

It's Friday. It's Halloween. It's the night that we will blow everyone's minds. No one is going to believe this. We will be famous. Kids are going to talk about this for years. Their kids will talk about it. Their kids' kids will talk about it.

I'm supposed to meet Frankie, Ramesh, and Monty at these doors. They should be here in exactly five minutes. We have everything planned right down to the minute.

4:41 p.m. Back doors of gym

Where are those guys? What are they doing? They have to lift a ramp into the back of a truck. How hard can that be? The teachers will be here soon to set up for the dance. If they don't make it here before then, the whole plan is shot.

4:46 p.m. — Back doors of gym

Still not here.

6:22 p.m. — Bedroom

Frankie, Ramesh, and Monty didn't show up until 5:01. The ramp was in the back of the truck. We all lifted it down. Ramesh said his mother asked where they were taking the ramp. He said to a skateboarding party. Good thing she bought that. We totally need that ramp.

We went to go in the back doors of the gym. They were locked.

"Crap!" I said.

"I can't believe this!" said Monty. "You guys didn't make sure the gym doors were open?" he yelled.

"But they're always open," said Frankie.

"Well, not tonight. Now what are you going to do?" Monty asked. He looked mad.

"I'll go in the front doors of the school. I'll open the gym doors from the inside," I said.

"You can't," said Frankie.

"Why not?" I said. It sounded like a good plan to me.

"Because Mrs. Berger and Mr. Sweet are out there talking. They'll see you go in and wonder what you're up to," said Ramesh.

"Shoot! This is never going to work. Come on guys. I'm taking this ramp back, and then I'm going home," said Monty.

"Wait!" I yelled. I pulled out the keys. There were still some mystery keys. I tried one of the keys in the gym doors. It didn't fit.

Then I tried the next one. It fit and turned. I pushed the big brown door open. Ha!

"Cool," said Frankie.

"Okay, let's do this," said Monty.

We tied the doors open. We all carefully lifted the ramp into the gym. The gym was dark and cool. There were orange and black streamers everywhere. The curtains on the stage were covered in fake cobwebs.

We set the ramp down on the gym floor. I unlocked the door under the stage.

There were stairs under the stage. I rolled the stairs out. We slid the ramp over the stairs. The ramp is just one big sheet of wood with wooden sides. It fit perfectly! We needed the stairs to keep the ramp from breaking in half. The ramp was strong enough to hold us. But if it broke in the middle of the plan, we'd be in big trouble. The plan would be shot.

Then Frankie and Monty went out into the parking lot. I waited in the gym. Ramesh waited just outside the doors as a lookout. I went backstage and pulled the string that opened the curtains. I walked back down the ramp to the floor. It seemed sturdy enough for the job.

ramp

I could hear voices in the hallway. I was getting nervous. The voices passed. We only had about twenty more minutes. The teachers would start coming in the gym soon to set up. I was wondering what was taking Frankie and Monty so long. I was getting kind of nervous. I had told Frankie where the keys were. Maybe he couldn't remember what I had said.

I was sure our plan wasn't going to work. Then Frankie and Monty came through. They just made it in the double doors in time. It was a tight fit. The noise rumbled through the gym. I thought for sure the teachers would hear something. Ramesh and I stood on either side of the ramp. We directed Monty where to go. He moved quickly and made it up onto the stage. We couldn't believe it.

Quickly, we closed the curtains. We moved the ramp off the stairs. We slid the stairs back under the stage. I locked them up. We all picked up a corner of the ramp. We carried it outside as quietly as we could. We lifted the ramp into the back of Monty's truck again. I shut the gym doors and locked them with the key. There was no going back now.

I said good-bye to the three of them. They had to drive the ramp back to Ramesh's place.

"See you in an hour and a half," I called to them. Monty waved as they drove out of the parking lot.

There's no way I'm dressing up as a pirate. There's just no way. I told Jason I would, but I've changed my mind. I look like a loser in that costume.

Trevor and Frankie are supposed to be dressing up as football players. Ramesh has a pair of glasses with a fake nose and mustache. His costume is a weird old man. He put it on last week when I was over at his house. Actually, he kind of looked like Mr. Sweet.

There's a prize for best costume. But I don't care. I tried on the pirate costume, and I felt like a nerd. It has a big white shirt with puffy arms. There are all these beads and a big red belt. As if! I'm just not wearing it.

I like the eye patch though.

Costume:

√ Black pants (I put my journal in the side pocket. I don't want to miss recording any of the plan.)

√ Black shirt with red paint smeared on the front.

√ White face. (I didn't have white makeup, so I patted flour on my face. It didn't really stick at first. I had to pour a big bowl of flour. Then I stuck my face in it.)

√ Black eyeliner smeared all around my eyes.

√ Mom's red lipstick in a line dripping down from my mouth.

√ To top it off, one eye patch.

So what am I? I don't even know. A one-eyed zombie I guess. Who bit his tongue. And the blood trickled down his chin and all over his shirt.

Good enough.

Boys bathroom — Third sink from the left.

Jason was pretty mad when he saw me in the front hall. He was all dressed up in his geeky pirate costume. He even had a red bandana tied around his head. Ramesh was there, too. He was wearing his fake nose and mustache. There were some other kids hanging around in the hall. They all had on dorky costumes.

Jason said, "Where is your pirate costume?"

I just said, "Uh, I don't know." I didn't know what else to say.

Then Trevor and Frankie showed up. They didn't have their football costumes on. They were also dressed all in black with zombie faces. We didn't even plan it that way.

Jason took off his bandana and stuffed it in his pocket. "You guys planned this!" he said.

"We didn't. Honest," I said.

"Hey, cool eye patch," Frankie said to me. That made Jason even madder.

74

"Yeah, that's because he's a pirate zombie," said Jason.

"What?" said Frankie.

Jason said, "Never mind."

Just then Suki and Ashley walked up to us. Suki was dressed like a cat. She had a long black tail and furry ears. Ashley was dressed like a genie. She had puffy pink pants and a short pink top. She was also wearing a pink belly ring. Her hair was in a ponytail on top of her head.

"Hi, guys, we're here," said Ashley.

I said, "Yeah, we can see that."

Then she said, "What are you supposed to be?"

I said, "A one-eyed zombie."

"So, maybe now you guys can tell us what the plan is," said Suki. The two girls stood there staring at us.

"Yeah…no," I said.

"This is your last chance," said Ashley.

"Our last chance to what? Tell you? Ha. We'll pass," I said.

"Yeah, we'll pass," said Trevor.

Then Ashley walked over and stood right beside me. Suki stood right beside Frankie. She put her arm around his. Frankie looked at her and grinned. Ashley put her arm around mine. I just stood there for a minute. What the—? I took my arm away and put my hands in my pockets.

Ashley turned to me. She said really sweetly, "Let's go, Nate."

What was she talking about? "What? Where?" I said.

Frankie cleared his throat really loudly. He slapped my arm and said, "Hey, Nate. I've got to tell you something. Come with me for a second."

I followed him into the boys' bathroom. I asked him what was going on. Were he and Suki dating now? Why did Ashley want us both to go everywhere with them?

"Uh, well, actually…you see…uh…" That was what he said. He couldn't even say it.

"What?" I asked.

"Remember the deal I made with Suki and Ashley? You know, so they would keep quiet about our plan?" he said.

"Yeah, what about it?" I knew where this was going and I didn't like it.

"Well, uh, the deal was." He cleared his throat. "The deal was that you would be Ashley's date for the dance."

"WHAT!" I yelled. I'm sure everyone out in the hall heard me.

"Well, I like Suki and Ashley likes you. I thought it would be a good deal," he said.

I couldn't believe it. "But I don't like Ashley," I said.

"You don't hate her," he said.

"No, but, but…" It was no use. They were waiting outside. It was a done deal. "Fine, but I'm not holding hands with her," I told him.

"Fine."

"And no slow dancing," I said.

"Fine."

"This can't get in the way of the plan," I said.

"It won't. That was also part of the deal. The girls have to respect the plan," Frankie said.

So now here I am in the bathroom, writing in this journal. There is a genie out there waiting for me. I hope she doesn't think I like her now. I don't want to spend the rest of grade eight being Ashley's boyfriend. And I REALLY don't want Miranda to think I like Ashley.

9 p.m. — Boys' bathroom

Operation: Hideout

Here I am again at the third sink from the left. This has been the longest night of my life. First of all, it's taking forever to get to nine-thirty. That's when we pull the prank. Second, there has been hand holding AND slow dancing.

Ashley just holds my hand when we're walking. Once, she yanked me onto the dance floor when slow music came on. What could I do? I wasn't going to run away. So I danced with her.

She put her arms around my neck. So I put my hands around her waist, and we started dancing. She kept mouthing things to her friends over my shoulder. Her ponytail kept hitting me in the face.

I kept a close eye on the stage the whole time. The music table was set up in front of the stage. The curtains had that cobweb stuff all over them. The soda and snacks table was by the front door. Fake spiders floated in the big bowl of soda.

The slow dance ended. Ashley and I went over to the soda table. She made me pour a drink into a cup for her. That's when I saw Miranda. She was dressed as a devil. She was wearing a red top, red shorts, red tights, and red shoes. She had a red tail, red horns, and a big red fork thing. She was wearing red lipstick. She looked really good.

"Hi," I said to Miranda.

"Hi," she said. I haven't talked to her since that time in music class. Her dark hair was curlier than usual.

"Do you want some soda, too?" I said.

"Sure," she said. So I got another cup and poured her some with the dipper. I handed it to her.

"Look, it's red too," I said. Duh! Why did I say that? Couldn't I think of anything better than that?

"Nate is a one-eyed ghoul," said Ashley. Ashley! I forgot all about her. She had her arms crossed in front of her. Her lips were pressed together. She looked annoyed.

"Actually, I'm a one-eyed zombie," I said.

Miranda smiled.

Ashley said, "Whatever. Let's go ask for a song, Nate."

Just then, Trevor walked up behind me.

"It's time," he said.

I looked at the girls. "Sorry, but I have to go," I said. I left them standing together by the drinks.

Mrs. Berger

Mrs. Berger

Mrs. Ber
Mrs. Berger

Mrs. Berger

Mrs. Berger

Mrs. Berger

Mrs. Berger

Mrs. Berger

Mrs. Berger

Mrs.

Mrs. Berger

Mrs. Berger

Midnight — My bedroom.

Operation: Final surprise!

You should have seen their faces!

I met up with Trevor, Jason, Frankie, and Ramesh in the bathroom. Ramesh had just thought of something. We had no way of opening the curtains. We couldn't do it ourselves. Someone else had to open them. Otherwise, the teachers would know it was us. But who? We didn't want to get anyone else in trouble. We also didn't want anybody to tell on us. Our whole plan was almost over. We all started yelling and blaming each other.

Then Frankie told us all to shut up. He had thought of a wicked idea. "We'll get one of the teachers to open them," he said.

"How are we going to do that?" asked Trevor. It was a good plan, but Trevor had a point. How could we get a teacher to open the curtains?

"We'll ask Miss Mirel to open them. We'll tell her there are more decorations behind it," said Jason.

But we didn't want to give ourselves away. We decided that there was only one way to do it. We had to write a fake note from the principal. Now things were getting tricky. If the teachers found out, we'd all be dead. Faking a teacher's writing is a big deal. Kids have gotten in big trouble for doing that.

Ramesh had some paper and a pen in his pocket. I ripped open my journal. We all practiced Mrs. Berger's handwriting. We had seen it enough times on our report cards. We all knew what it looked like. The guys decided that mine was the closest. So I ripped out a piece of paper. In my neatest, girliest handwriting I wrote:

I have planned a surprise for the students. Please open the curtains when I turn on the lights.

Mrs. Berger

Then I folded it up into a square.

We decided to have the note passed to Miss Mirel. She was running the DJ table beside the stage. It would make sense for her to open the curtains.

But whoever gave it to her would get in trouble. We decided to put the note on the CD player. We could do it while Miss Mirel wasn't looking. She would just think that Mrs. Berger had left it there.

We didn't want to look like we were up to something. So, one by one, we walked back into the dark gym.

There was dance music on. A bunch of kids were dancing in a big circle. I started walking over to the music table. Ashley saw me and ran up beside me. For once, I didn't mind that she took my hand. It made me look like just another person at the dance.

"Stand with me by the music table for a minute," I said.

"Why?" she said.

"You can't ask questions. It's part of the plan," I said.

She said, "Oh." She smiled. I think she was glad to finally be a part of the plan.

So we stood by the music table for a bit. I pretended to look at the binders of CDs. Miss Mirel bent down to get another binder. I tossed the note onto the CD player. Then I pulled Ashley out onto the dance floor. We joined the circle with all the other kids. I pretended to dance. That's how I dance anyway. I can't do it. I just pretend.

I had my back to the music table. I leaned over toward Ashley. Then I whispered, "What is Miss Mirel doing?"

"Nothing," she said into my ear.

"How about now?" I said again.

"Still nothing," she said. We danced for what seemed like an hour.

"Oh, wait! I think she just saw the note," said Ashley.

"Yeah? What's she doing?" I asked. I peeked around. I didn't want to look like I was watching her.

"She's opening it...now she's reading it...now she's looking around," Ashley said.

I looked around, too. I saw Trevor and Frankie standing by the front door. Jason and Ramesh were also on the dance floor. At least I wasn't the only one suffering.

I looked at Frankie. I nodded my head and pulled on my ear. It was our secret sign. Frankie inched closer to the door where all the lights were. He waited until a group of kids was walking through the doors. He turned on all the lights with one flip of his hand. Then he joined the group of people as they walked into the gym.

Everyone in the gym stopped dancing. They covered their eyes as the bright light flooded the dark room. The music was still playing.

"Who turned on the lights?" some kid yelled.

Miss Mirel left the music table and climbed onto the stage. She reached back and pulled the rope that opened the curtains.

I looked at Frankie and Trevor. They were grinning from ear to ear. I must have been, too.

Everyone noticed that Miss Mirel was on the stage. All eyes were on the curtains as she jerked them open. I kept my eyes on the crowd of kids. I wanted to see the looks on their faces.

First there was complete stillness and quiet. Then there were a few hoots and shouts. Some kids clapped a little. Most just laughed really loudly. Within about thirty seconds, everyone was cheering wildly.

I caught sight of Mrs. Berger. She had walked into the middle of the gym. She just stood there staring at the stage. Everyone was looking at her and then at the stage. She looked really mad.

We did it! My heart was pounding. I couldn't believe the plan had worked.

There was Mrs. Berger looking at the stage. I knew what she was seeing. Her tiny little car was parked in the middle of it.

"Who did this?" she yelled. No one answered her. Mr. Sweet rushed over to her. "Who did this?" she asked him. He just shook his head.

"The dance is over!" Mrs. Berger yelled. "Everybody has to go home!" No one really moved at all. Everyone was too busy talking to each other and pointing to the stage.

That's when I turned around to look at the stage. I wanted to see our perfect prank. It was just as wicked as I expected. But...

Something above Mrs. Berger's car caught my eye. It was my gym T-shirt. It was hanging from a string across the stage above the car. Hanging beside it were my gym shoes. Other things were hanging from the string.

Ramesh's shoes and Jason's sweatshirt. Socks, baseball caps, a bag, and even a bathing suit.

"Hey, those are my jeans," said Frankie.

"That's my bag," Trevor called out.

"And that's my shirt," said Ramesh.

I looked around. Suki and Ashley were staring right at me. They both smiled and waved. Suki reached into her pocket and pulled out a piece of paper. She unfolded it and held it up for me to see. It was the list of names. Each one had a check mark beside it.

Suki and Ashley both mouthed the word "Gotcha" at the same time. They gave each other a high five.

After all that work, the dumb girls had the last laugh. It was a prank on us and only us. It had a clear message. They've been on to us right from the beginning. The thing is, I can't figure out how they found out what our plan was.

Well, at least our prank still kicked theirs. The principal's car! On the stage! Kids are going to be talking about it for years to come. Their kids will talk about it. Their kids' kids will talk about it. Who cares about a bunch of hanging gym clothes? Well, besides us.

I guess the moral of this story is: watch out for girls. You can like them. You can write them notes. You can even think they look good in red. Just watch out.

Oh yeah, and there's one more thing. Never leave your stuff lying around.

Glossary

allen key
A small tool for tightening or loosening screws

amateur
A person who lacks experience

badminton
A sport played with rackets in which a birdie is hit
back and forth over a net

belly
The stomach

bracelet
A piece of jewelry that is worn on the wrist

coach
A person who teaches a sports team

costume
An outfit to wear for dress up

curtains
Drapes

detention
A punishment that involves staying late
after school

dribble
To bounce a basketball rapidly

eye patch
A piece of material that covers up one eye

flute
A long wooden or metal instrument that is played
by blowing into a mouth-hole at one end of it

garage
A building used to shelter cars and trucks

genie
A magical spirit that grants wishes

ghoul
An evil being that robs graves

glove box
A small storage compartment in the dashboard of a car

highlighter
A neon-colored marker

hoops
A slang term for a practice game of basketball

janitor
A caretaker who looks after a school

mirror
A surface on which you can see your reflection

pantsed
To have one's pants pulled down in public

pirate
An old-fashioned criminal who sailed the high seas and stole from other ships

prank
A practical joke

ramp

A short wooden structure that slants upward

saxophone

A large brass wind instrument

slam

To shut with loud force

sneeze

To cough suddenly

Tamaguchi

A small electronic game that involves taking care of a small character

tissue

A piece of soft, thin paper used for blowing your nose

trumpet

A brass wind instrument with a bell-shaped end

zombie

A being that has come back from the dead

Other books by K.E. Calder and Tea Leaf Press

Spend the summer with Mel Randall and Will Bergeron! The novels in the **Deer Lake** series follow the summer cottage adventures of two young teens and their group of friends.

Summer of Change by H.J. Lewis

Every year, Mel Randall can't wait to spend the summer at Deer Lake. But not this summer. Mel's best friend has moved away. The general store has new owners. Everything is changing. Then Mel has an adventure and meets Ian Suwan. Maybe a little change isn't so bad after all.

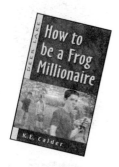

How to be a Frog Millionaire by K.E. Calder

Will Bergeron is stuck at his grandma's cottage for the whole summer. To make matters worse, his bratty twin cousins are there, too. Will is the only guy his age without a summer job. He comes up with a plan to make money. Will just has to hope his grandma doesn't find out.
ISBN 1-55068-126-5

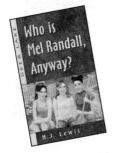

Who is Mel Randall, Anyway? by H.J. Lewis

Mel Randall's new neighbor, Diana, is nothing like Mel. Diana cares more about clothes, nail polish, and magazines. She gives Mel a makeover. Mel's friend, Allison, likes the old Mel. Diana's cute brother, Ted, likes the new Mel. The question is: who is the real Mel Randall?
ISBN 1-55068-128-1

The Stalker by K.E. Calder

A dark figure on a stormy night. A set of lost keys. A body bag. No one knows how old Beatrice Jones disappeared from Deer Lake. All the clues point to Booker. He's the grumpy old man in the cottage next door. Can Will prove that Booker is a murderer? Or will he become Booker's next victim?
ISBN 1-55068-124-9

Stranded by K.E. Calder

The worst has happened. Will is trapped at a cottage with Mel Randall and her two sisters. How will he survive for two whole weeks? Living in a house full of girls is more than Will expected. He has a secret to keep from Mel. Will he tell her when they become lost on a dark, foggy night?
ISBN 1-55068-122-2

The Secret of the Bailey Bay Inn by K.E. Calder

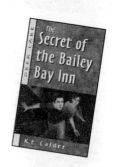

Weird things are happening at the Bailey Bay Inn. The old hotel is boarded up. It has been deserted for years. Or has it? Will does some research on the run-down building. He learns the truth about its terrible past. Now are Will and his friends in danger?
ISBN 1-55068-097-8

The Accidental Camper by H.J. Lewis

A canoe trip, a cool counselor, and her best friends. Life can't get much better than this. Except for a few small details. Mel fights with her boyfriend; her two friends can't stand each other; and Diana doesn't know one end of a canoe paddle from the other. It's going to take all of Mel's resources to survive this trip!
ISBN 1-55068-119-2

For more information, visit www.tealeafpress.com

Special Thanks

Jane Lewis, Hannelore Sotzek, April Fast,
Heather Evoy, Ben Kooter, Shawn Evoy,
Sam Turton, John Evoy, and Ron Fast.